HELLO BABY!

for Nicholas Harlow Alcorn
April 18, 1989
9 pounds 3 ounces
and
Nigel John Alcorn
May 13, 1992
7 pounds 3 ounces

With special thanks to Melanie Marin, M.D.,
for her expert advice and to the Marsh family, especially Max.

HELLO BABY!

PLEASE CHECK IN

LIZZY ROCKWELL

DRAGONFLY BOOKS — NEW YORK

All rights reserved. Published in the United States by Dragonfly Books, an imprint of Random House Children's Books,
a division of Random House, Inc., New York. Originally published in hardcover in the United States by
Alfred A. Knopf, an imprint of Random House Children's Books, a division of Random House, Inc., New York, in 1999.

Dragonfly Books with the colophon is a registered trademark of Random House, Inc.

Visit us on the Web! **www.randomhouse.com/kids**

Educators and librarians, for a variety of teaching tools, visit us at
www.randomhouse.com/teachers

Library of Congress Cataloging-in-Publication Data
Rockwell, Lizzy.
Hello baby! / Lizzy Rockwell.
p.   cm.
Summary: A young boy describes how a new baby is growing inside his mommy and tells what it is like when
his new sister comes home from the hospital.
ISBN 978-0-517-80011-9 (trade) — ISBN 978-0-517-80012-6 (lib. bdg.) — ISBN 978-0-517-80074-4 (pbk.)
[1. Babies—Fiction. 2. Brothers and sisters—Fiction.] I. Title.
PZ7.R59486Ou 1999
98007339 [E]—dc21

MANUFACTURED IN CHINA

16 15 14 13 12 11 10 9 8 7

I sit very still. I wait, and I wait—then I feel it! Kind of like a swoosh and kind of like a thump, it's almost nothing at all. But I know that funny feeling. It's our baby! Hello, baby!

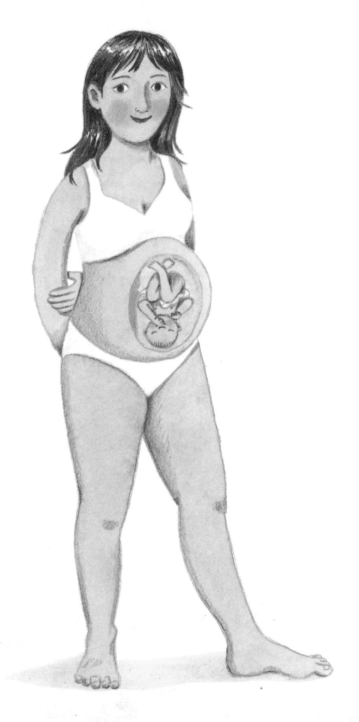

In Mommy's body, in a place called the womb, a baby is growing. It floats in a dark, warm sac of water. It hears Mommy's heartbeat, voices, and sounds from the world outside.

An umbilical cord brings everything a baby needs to grow. Our baby doesn't use its mouth to eat or breathe, but it practices. It sucks its tiny thumb and fills and empties its lungs with water to make them strong.

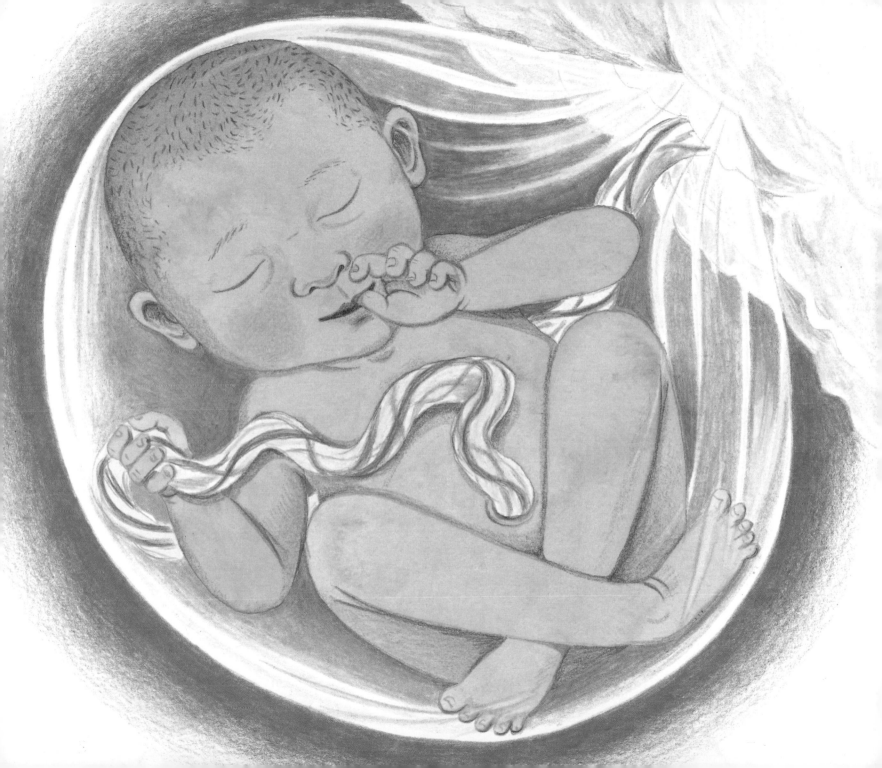

In the examining room, Mommy gets
measured and weighed. Dr. Marin's careful
hands show us where our baby's head
and feet are. We listen to the heartbeat.
Pah-pum, pah-pum, pah-pum. It's loud
and steady and faster than mine.

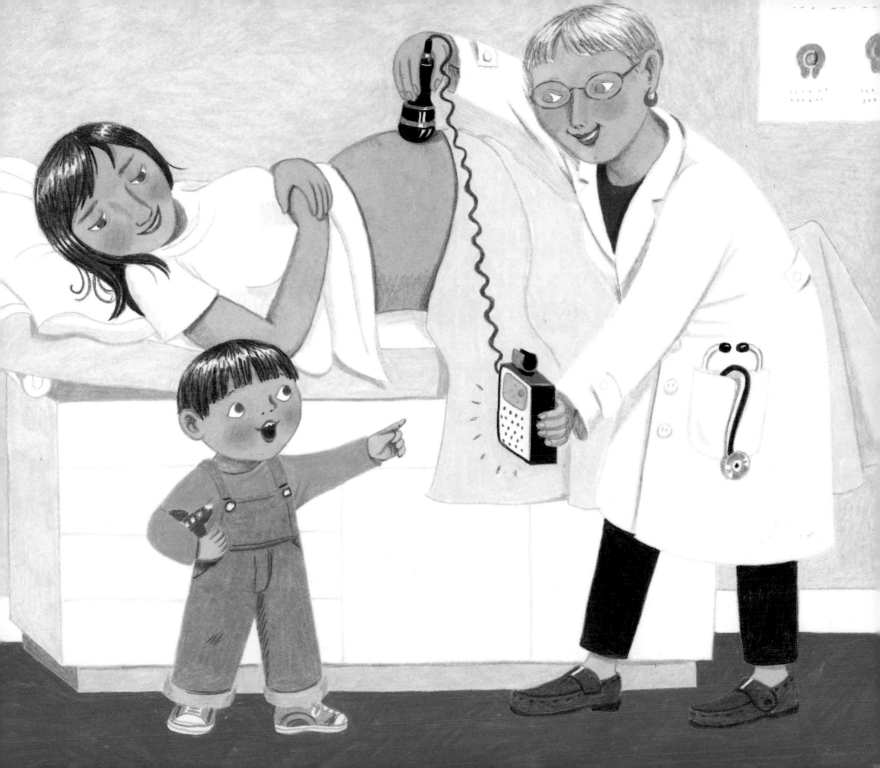

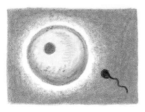

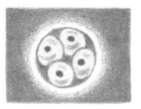

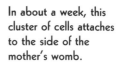

In about a week, this cluster of cells attaches to the side of the mother's womb.

A tiny egg cell from the mother is fertilized by a tiny sperm cell from the father.

After a day, the fertilized cell splits in half, forming two cells.

These two cells each split—now there are four cells.

After a few days, a cluster of cells has formed.

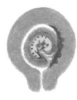

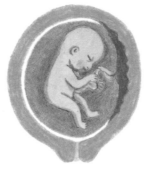

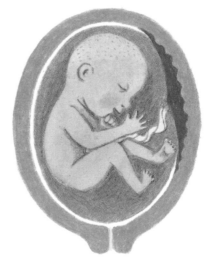

8 weeks

Cells have begun to take a human form. Head, eyes, and spine can be seen. Arms and legs are tiny bumps.

12 weeks

All body parts are now formed, including toes, fingers, and eyelids.

16 weeks

Fetus begins to exercise lungs. Can hear and grasp. Eyes are shut.

24 weeks

Fat begins to form under the skin. With room to move, fetus is very active.

On a chart, we see how a baby grows. At first it's so small you can't see it without a microscope. Now Mommy is 32 weeks pregnant.

OW A BABY GROWS

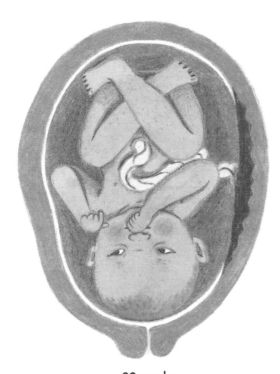

32 weeks

Toenails and fingernails
have formed. Eyes can
open and close. Soft
fuzz covers the body.

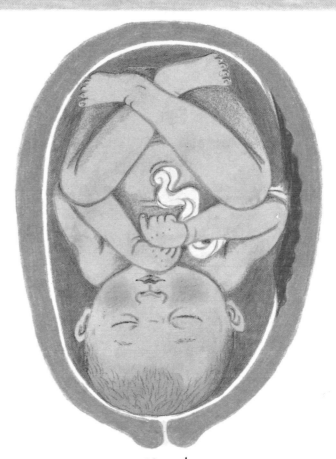

40 weeks

Lungs are fully formed.
Skin is soft and smooth.
Baby is plump and
ready to be born.

Our baby has eyes that can open, fingernails, toenails, and soft fuzz all over. Only
eight more weeks and our baby will be ready to be born. Soon I will be a brother.

We are getting ready. We unpack tiny socks, hats, and onesies—the clothes that I wore. I find a soft ball with a key. I crank the key and listen. Hey! I know that song.

One morning I wake up early. I hear footsteps and voices. Grannie is here!

Our baby is ready. It's time for Daddy to take Mommy to the hospital. Grannie and I kiss them good-bye. I'm sad to see them go. But Mommy says that at the hospital Dr. Marin and the nurses will help our baby be born. Just like they helped me.

Grannie says she will never forget the day I was born. She
unfolds our favorite pictures from her wallet.

We can't believe how big I have grown.

Grannie and I bake cookies and draw pictures. We build a fort and have
our lunch inside. Suddenly, the phone rings. It's Daddy with good news.
Our baby is born!

We call her Eliza. She is very tiny. But in my lap she feels heavy and warm. Her neck is weak, so I hold up her head. Her hands are strong. She grabs my finger tight and doesn't let go. Hello, Eliza!

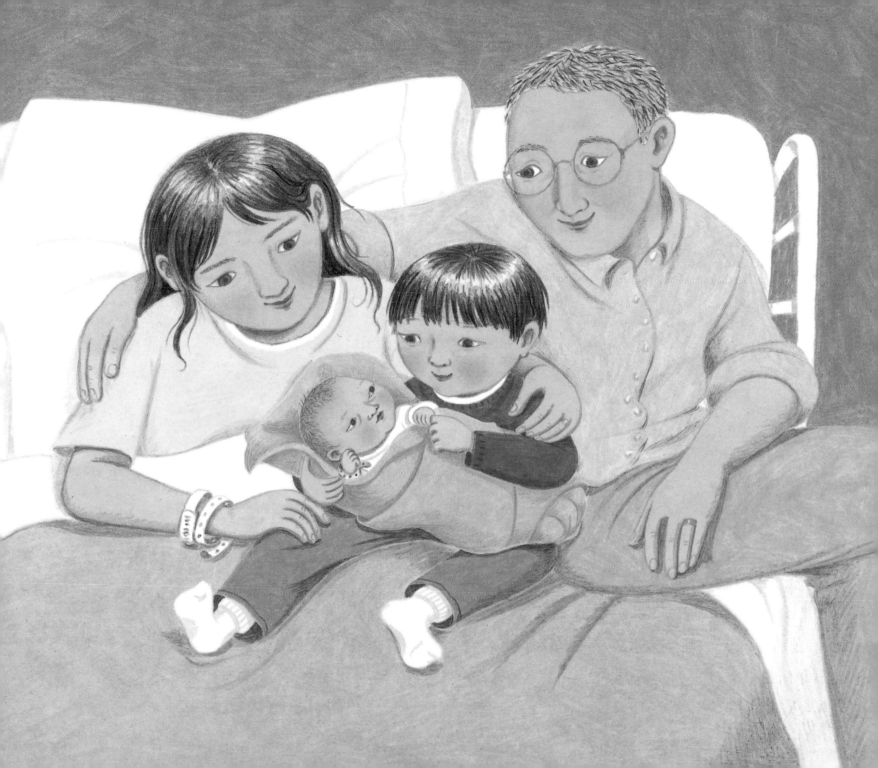

After two days, Mommy and Eliza come home. The house is filled with flowers and presents. Right aw Eliza is hungry. She sounds like a ca when she cries. Mommy nurses her the rocker. Mommy's breasts make n that is the perfect food for a baby. Soon Eliza falls asleep in her lap.

Our baby sleeps a lot. She doesn't understand about daytime and nighttime. In the womb it was dark, but soon she will learn. I watch her sleep for a while. Then I go play. Someday my sister will play with me.

When Eliza wakes up, Daddy and I give her a sponge bath. We wipe off her whole body and head with warm water from a bowl. We are careful of the soft spot on top of her head. We wipe around the black scab on her stomach. That's where the umbilical cord was. Soon the scab will fall off and Eliza will have a belly button like me.

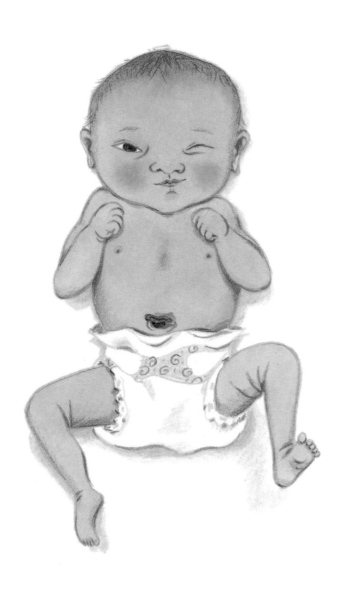

We put on her diaper.

An undershirt that snaps.

Tiny socks.

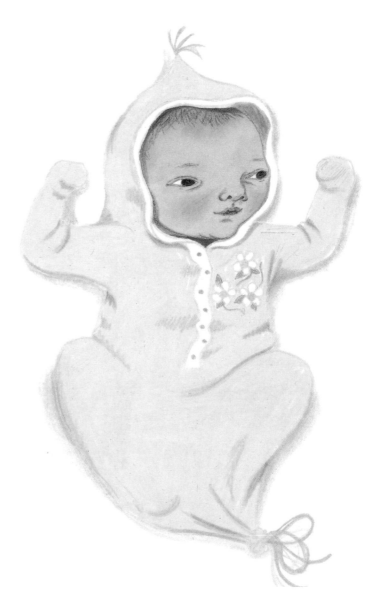

Then a sleeper with mittens and a hood.

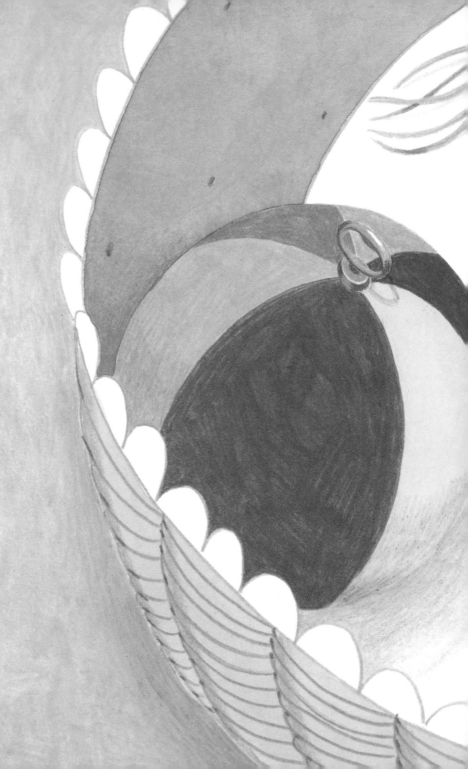

Eliza eats again and lets out a huge
burp. But she doesn't fall asleep.
Instead, she starts crying. Not like a cat
this time. Angry sounds like a police
siren. She spits up, too. Daddy tries
patting her back. Mommy lays her in
her basket and rubs her tummy. But
Eliza doesn't stop crying.

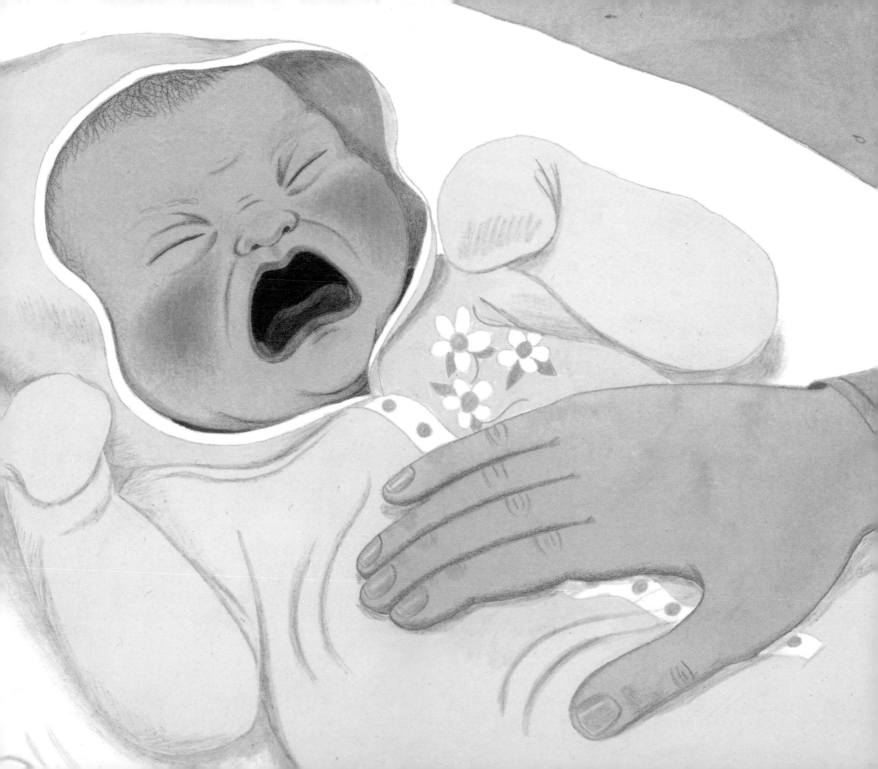

Then I remember the ball. I wind the key, and it starts to
play. Eliza is surprised. She is so surprised she stops crying
to listen. Mommy and Daddy sing the words to that song.
Soon Eliza looks sleepy.

It's been a big day. Our baby came home.